Sit in!

Written by Clare Helen Welsh

Illustrated by Julia Seal

Collins

Sit in Sam.

2

Sam sits in.

3

Sit in Sid.

Sid sits in.

Sit in Nad.

Nad sits in.

7

Sit in Pam.

Sit in Tam.

Pam sits in.

Tam sits in.

Sit in Sam.

Sam sits in.

/n/

14

🐾 Review: After reading 🐾

Use your assessment from hearing the children read to choose any GPCs, words or tricky words that need additional practice.

Read 1: Decoding

- Say the word **Sit** on page 6. Ask the children to say it too, encouraging them to sound out each letter (s/i/t) first, then blending.
- Turn to page 10 and ask the children to sound out **sits** (s/i/t/s) and then blend.
- On pages 12 and 13, focus on the words **sit** and **sits**. Ask the children to sound out and blend these two words, checking they don't forget the additional /s/ in **sits**.
- Look at the "I spy sounds" pages (14–15). Point to the nose of the boy near the mirror and say: "nose", emphasising the /n/ sound. Ask the children to find more things that contain the /n/ sound. (*nurse, necklace, numbers, nine, net, neck, notepad, nap, noise, notes, noticeboard, noodles*) Point out how some things might have the /n/ in the middle or at the end. (e.g. *sniff, dance, pan, sun, wand*)

Read 2: Prosody

- Model reading each page with expression to the children. After you have read each page, ask the children to have a go at reading with expression.
- On pages 4, 6 and 8, show children how you read Sam's words in a friendly way as she invites her friends to sit in the car.
- Take turns to use a different voice for the narrator.

Read 3: Comprehension

- For every question ask the children how they know the answer. Ask:
  - On pages 6 and 7, how do you know that "Nad" is a name? (e.g. *it has a capital letter*)
  - On pages 8 and 9, why is Sam getting out? (e.g. *to make room for Pam and Tam*)
  - How is Sam feeling on page 10? (e.g. *she feels sad as she isn't in the car*)
  - Does the story have a happy ending? Why? (e.g. *It has a happy ending because all the children are in the car and they are smiling.*)